Sally's Homework

Om KIDZ

An imprint of Om Books International

First Published in 2023

Om Kidz | Om Books International

Corporate & Editorial Office
A-12, Sector 64, Noida 201 301
Uttar Pradesh, India
Phone: +91 120 477 4100
Email: editorial@ombooks.com
Website: www.ombooksinternational.com

Sales Office
107, Ansari Road, Darya Ganj
New Delhi 110 002, India
Phone: +91 11 4000 9000
Email: sales@ombooks.com

ISBN: 978-93-94547-38-4

Printed in India

10 9 8 7 6 5 4 3 2 1

Sally's Homework

I'm all set to read

Paste your photograph here

My name is

Sally was **sitting** at her **computer**. It was a Sunday, but she had some homework to complete.

Her Mom had gone to visit her sick granny. **Sally** was alone **with** her **Dad**.

“Let’s go out somewhere, **Sally**,” **said Dad**.
“I need to **write** an essay on transportation, **Dad**,” **said Sally**.

"Come along, let's go for a **walk**. You can finish this once we return," **said Dad**.

Sally happily skipped along **with Dad**. Suddenly, she spotted a **car**. “This **car** is so old-fashioned. I wonder if it still runs,” **said Sally**.

"Ah! That one is a vintage **car**, **Sally**. It belongs to Mr. Dash, my friend. He must be taking this to the Vintage **Car** Rally!"

"What is a vintage **car**, **Dad**?" asked **Sally**.

"They are **cars** from olden **times**. Some people like to collect very old **cars**. They keep them as good as new," explained **Dad**.

"Just like I collect old coins!" cried **Sally**.

"Yes. Such people **then** get together and showcase these **cars** in a rally.

You will see many such **cars** in the rally," **said Dad**. "Look! Here go two more..."

"Why don't I see vintage **cars** every day, **Dad**?" asked **Sally**. **Dad** smiled and explained, "These old **cars** need a lot of petrol to run.

They cause a lot of pollution too. Also, they cannot match up to the speed of **cars** you see today. So, they are kept off the roads, except during such rallies."

"**Sally** wants to go to the rally," sang **Sally**. She clapped and danced saying, "See how it rhymes, **Dad**!

Sally-rally, **Sally**-rally!" **Dad laughed**. Soon they reached the Transport Museum. "**Would** you like to go inside, **Sally**?" asked **Dad**. "Sure **Dad**!" shouted **Sally with** joy.

"It all started **with** the invention of the **wheel**, you know," **said Dad**. "**Cars**, motorbikes, bicycles, buses, trucks, scooters, rickshaws, carts – they all run on **wheels**."

BUS

“Not all things run on **wheels** though,” **Dad** continued. “Can you name a few things that do not need **wheels** to run?”

"A train!" cried **Sally**, as her eyes fell upon a **huge** model of a train standing at the platform.

"Trains run on tracks,
but they do have **wheels**.
Look!" **said Dad**.

"Umm… a **boat**… a hot-air balloon… a ski?" tried **Sally**.

Now they had reached the section where **other** modes of transport were displayed.

"Animals too are used to pull carts on **wheels** to carry loads and people," **said Dad**, pointing towards a **village** scene **which** displayed **bullocks pulling** a **fruit** cart.

"Oh yes! I remember **Pete** used to deliver watermelons from his farm in his **donkey** cart. And I used to think it was a baby **horse** who **refused** to grow up!" **laughed Sally**.

"And it **would** bray every **time** I honked the **horn** on my **car**," **laughed Dad**.

"Look at the **horn** on that **car**," **said Sally**. "This one looks so different from our **car**. Where are the seat belts?"

Dad laughed aloud. “Old **cars** did not have all these things, **Sally**,” he explained.

“There were no ACs, no music systems, and no seat belts back **then**. Hey, it’s **time** for the rally. Let’s go!”

“This is awesome, **Dad**!”

"I am so glad you **brought** me here," cried an excited **Sally**.

After returning home, **Sally completed** her homework **with** the help of the photographs **Dad** had **clicked** for her. It was a joyful day for **Sally**.

She **would** always cherish the memories.

Know Your Words

Sight Words

brought	other	walk	would
fruit	then	which	write
huge	time	with	

Naming Words

Sally	car	horse	dad
computer	horn	Pete	donkey
bullock	boat	village	wheels

Doing Words

sitting	laughed	said
clicked	completed	
refused	pulling	